# Cat's Very Good Day

words by
## Kristen Tracy

pictures by
## David Small
CALDECOTT MEDALIST

putnam

**G. P. PUTNAM'S SONS**

## G. P. PUTNAM'S SONS

An imprint of Penguin Random House LLC, New York

First published in the United States of America by G. P. Putnam's Sons, an imprint of Penguin Random House LLC, 2023

Visit us online at penguinrandomhouse.com.

Library of Congress Cataloging-in-Publication Data
Names: Tracy, Kristen, 1972– author. | Small, David, illustrator. | Title: Cat's very good day / by Kristen Tracy; illustrated by David Small.
Description: New York: G. P. Putnam's Sons, 2023. | Summary: A mischievous house cat has an eventful day full of relaxation and play.
Identifiers: LCCN 2021054028 (print) | LCCN 2021054029 (ebook) | ISBN 9781984815200 (hardcover) | ISBN 9781984815217 (epub)
ISBN 9781984815224 (kindle edition) | Subjects: CYAC: Stories in rhyme. | Cats—Fiction. | LCGFT: Picture books. | Stories in rhyme.
Classification: LCC PZ8.3.T663 Cat 2023 (print) | LCC PZ8.3.T663 (ebook) | DDC [E]—dc23
LC record available at https://lccn.loc.gov/2021054028
LC ebook record available at https://lccn.loc.gov/2021054029

Manufactured in China

ISBN 9781984815200
10 9 8 7 6 5 4 3 2 1
TOPL

Design by Nicole Rheingans | Text set in ITC Stone Informal Pro
The art was done digitally.

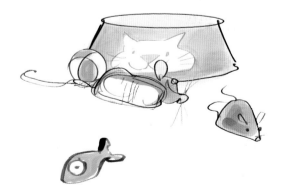

For Brian,
forever and always
and then some —K.T.

For Lily and Sarah —D.S.

Sunrise
lounger.

Piano-key
pounder.

Dollhouse fiddler.

Toilet-bowl dribbler.

Mirror attacker.

Morning-tea whacker.

What a
**lovely**
day.

Sock-drawer
slinker.

**Keyboard tinkerer.**

Potted-plant disaster.

Acrobat master.

Vacuum avoider.

Sofa destroyer.

What a
**happy**
day.

# Tightrope walker.

**Neighborhood stalker.**

Baby-squirrel chaser.

Mama-squirrel facer.

Rooftop
runner.

Welcome-mat
sunner.

What a
**wild**
day.

**Fishbowl tapper.**

Shoe-box napper.

Bottle-cap flicker.

Full-body licker.

**Hamster-ball snagger.**

**Hairball gagger.**

What a
**busy**
day.

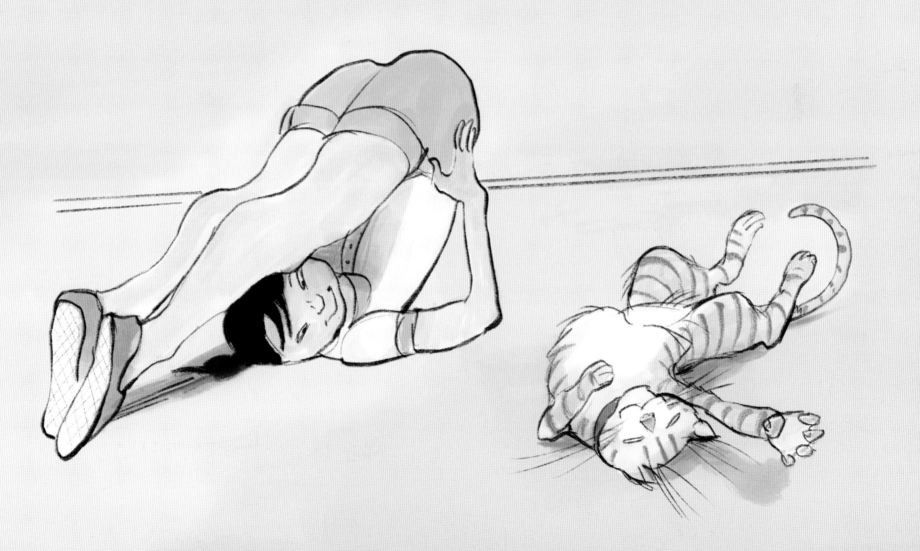

# Windowsill bounder.

Big-moon
sounder.

Dark-storm
worrier.

Back-closet
scurrier.

Curled-up loner.

Scaredy-cat
groaner.

What a **stressful** day.

**Bedtime sneaker.**

Warm-pillow seeker.

Half-asleep
schemer.

Stretched-out
dreamer.

Moonlight cuddler.

All-night snuggler.

What a very good day.